Marcus Sedgwick

Cudweed in Outer Space

Illustrated by Pete Williamson

Orion
Children's Books

First published in Great Britain in 2012
by Orion Children's Books
a division of the Orion Publishing Group Ltd
Orion House
5 Upper St Martin's Lane
London WC2H 9EA
An Hachette UK Company

1 3 5 7 9 10 8 6 4 2

A catalogue record for this book is available from the British Library.

ISBN 978 1 4440 0483 0

Printed in China

www.orionbooks.co.uk
www.ravenmysteries.co.uk

For Tamara (Marcus Sedgwick)

*For Alice Ballard - a book for big school
(Pete Williamson)*

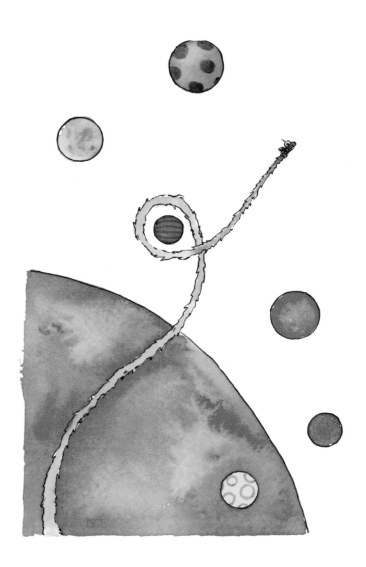

CONTENTS

CHAPTER 1

This is Cudweed.

If you think *he* looks funny, you should see his mum

and his dad.

He has a big sister too, and she looks like this, almost normal.

Almost.

If you think they all look a bit odd, you'd be right, but then, this is where they live.

And you couldn't live in a crazy castle like that and be normal, could you?

It's the sort of place where **odd** and **strange** things happen. A lot.
This is the story of what happened one day when Cudweed decided to read a comic…

Now, you might think that it would be hard to get into trouble by reading a comic. Yes?

No! Not if your name is Cudweed Yessir Frilly-Frou Derek Goatfeet Otherhand.

Cudweed had found the comic in an old box in the attic. It was called Rocket Boy, and it looked like this:

Cudweed read about the
AMAZING AND INCREDIBLE
ADVENTURES OF ROCKET
BOY. Rocket Boy got up to all sorts
of tricks, was ALWAYS in danger,
but always escaped by the end of
each story.

Cudweed thought Rocket Boy was cool. Soon he started thinking that he was Rocket Boy himself!

The thing that Cudweed liked best about Rocket Boy was Rocket Boy's spaceship.

It was so cool, Cudweed decided it was as cold as Absolute Zero, which, in a story called *Rocket Boy and the Thrillons of Zoy*, was the coldest possible temperature ever.

The spaceship looked like this:

But then a bad thing happened!
Cudweed finished reading the comic.
He didn't know what to do. So he
read it again.

Three hours later he had finished it again. And again, and again, until at last, he knew the whole thing from back to front and back again.

Cudweed felt sad and bored and worried, all at the same time.

Then, at the very back, he saw some adverts, trying to sell things, so he read them too.

And that was when he saw it.

BUILD YOUR OWN SPACESHIP KIT.

Easy assembly, suitable for 8 years and up. Allow 4-8 weeks for delivery. Price £5.

Cudweed asked his dad if he could have £5 to send away for the spaceship kit.

'What's that, my boy?' said his dad. 'Don't pester me, can't you see I'm busy trying to invent something here?'

'But, Dad, I just want to send off for this spaceship kit… It's just like Rocket Boy's.'

Cudweed's dad wasn't listening. Not properly.

So he put his hand in his pocket and gave Cudweed a £5 note.

'Off you go,' he said.

Cudweed grinned from ear to ear.

He sent off for the kit.

And four to eight weeks later, a very large box arrived...

CHAPTER 2

Cudweed looked at the box and almost fainted with excitement.

The box was a bit battered and
looked as though it had been sitting
in the corner of a forgotten store
room for a long time, but Cudweed
didn't mind.

On the side of the box was a picture of Rocket Boy standing with his space helmet under his arm and his spaceship behind him.

He had that look on his face. Sort of fearless and determined.

Cudweed stared at the picture for about another ten seconds and then tore his way into the box.

The first thing he found was a large page of instructions.

'Won't be needing those,' he said, and threw the page over his shoulder.

'I know exactly what Rocket Boy's spaceship looks like already.'

Just then Fellah, Cudweed's pet monkey, turned up and began to 'help' Cudweed by pulling all the pieces out of the box.

Very soon there was
a mess on Cudweed's
bedroom floor and it
didn't look much like
a rocket.

Cudweed sighed.

'Maybe I do need that page of instructions after all,' he said. But it was somewhere under the pieces of the rocket, nowhere to be seen.

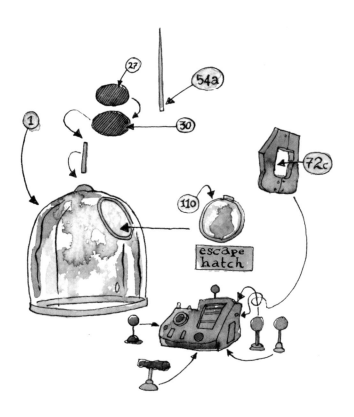

'Oh well,' he said, 'I'll just have to do my best. Fellah, would you hand me that spanner?'

So Cudweed began to build the rocket.

There were some bits that looked like this:

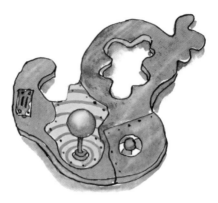

And forty-three bits that looked like this:

There was a large steering wheel that looked like this:

And this:

Cudweed banged and stuck and
sawed and hammered and drilled,
and four and a half hours later,
the rocket looked like this:

'Fellah,' said Cudweed, 'I'm not sure
that I have got it right.'

But he didn't give up, and after lunch, Cudweed did some more banging and hammering, and three hours after that the spaceship was finished.

'Coo,' said Cudweed. 'I've built a spaceship.'

He looked at Fellah.

'Shall we,' he whispered, 'go somewhere..?'

Fellah looked worried.

'Good!' shouted Cudweed. 'Let's go!'

And, handing Fellah the spare space helmet, they climbed aboard.

Cudweed pressed a large button marked **GO**.

Nothing happened.

Nothing happened for about three seconds, and then, with the most mighty whoosh, they were gone!

Whoosh!

Out of the bedroom window… and into space.

CHAPTER 3

Space turned out to be big.

In fact, space turned out to be very big.

'Well, Fellah,' said Cudweed. 'What do you think? Big, isn't it?'

Fellah said nothing. He had been very quiet since they had blasted into space, and kept looking out of the window.

'I wonder,' said Cudweed, 'what Rocket Boy does when he's in space.'

Fellah said nothing.

'I wonder if he, you know, ever gets, well... bored?'

This was a question which Cudweed never got an answer to. The next second there was a big bang and the rocket shook as if it had been hit by a missile.

Cudweed looked out the window, and screamed.

'Fellah! We've been hit by a missile!'

It was true.

Cudweed could see a spaceship that looked just like the one that belonged to the Thrillons of Zoy from the comic.

They were so close, he could even
see the Thrillons waving from the
window of their ship.

Then Cudweed realised that they
weren't waving. They were shaking
their tentacles at him, in an angry sort
of way.

Another missile zoomed out of the
Thrillon ship.

'Aaaargh!' wailed Cudweed, and
began to press every button on the
control panel in front of him.

The missile was about to hit them. Cudweed pressed one more button and the spaceship shot forward as if he had pushed a super turbo thrust button, which he had.

Cudweed and Fellah watched as the Thrillon missile hit a nearby asteroid and exploded on that instead.

But they weren't out of trouble. They were moving fast, very fast, and Cudweed couldn't control the ship any more.

Fellah screeched.

They were charging towards a large planet at high speed.

'I can't stop it!' howled Cudweed. 'It's gone crazy!'

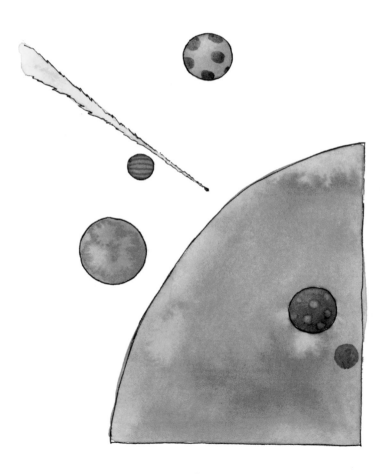

Moments later they crash-landed on
the surface of the planet, which was
soft and gooey. But not so soft that
the ship wasn't badly damaged.

'We're alive!' cried Cudweed, and since the window of the space ship was covered in goo, he opened the top hatch to have a look around.

'I hope they are friendly here,' he said, as he climbed out of the hatch.

Inside his space helmet, Cudweed went pale.

All around their ship were aliens, with many tentacles, and they were all pointing laser guns at him.

'Err, Fellah,' said Cudweed. 'I think I know where we are. It's possible, just possible, that we've crashed on Planet Zoy. Where the Thrillons come from.'

CHAPTER 4

One of the Thrillons, who looked like the meanest, stepped forward and waved a tentacle or two at Cudweed.

Cudweed guessed he was the King.

'Rargle roogle roo-rargle,'

he said.

Cudweed thought about this.

'In films,' he said, 'aliens always speak English. Really good English, in fact. Are you sure you don't speak English? Maybe you've just forgotten that you do.'

'Roogle roo-rargle rangle-roo,' said the Thrillon King, and blasted the side of Cudweed's ship with his laser gun.

It looked even less like it would ever be able to fly them home.

Fellah shot into the air. He landed on the top of the ship, and gawped at the Thrillons.

When they saw him all the Thrillons suddenly got down on their knees, if tentacles actually have knees. They began to make low noises, as if they were worshipping Fellah.

'Roo-rargle,' said the Thrillon King.
'Roo-rangle!'

They put down their guns and started
smiling at Cudweed instead.

Fellah gave a little screech, and the Thrillon King spoke again.

'Ringle-rargle. Roo-ringle-ringle. Roo?'

Fellah squawked, and the Thrillons began to rush around, and started to fix their spaceship.

Cudweed looked very puzzled.

'Fellah, are the Thrillons speaking monkey-language? Have you asked them to mend our spaceship so we can get home, and to not blast us into pieces, as well?'

Fellah scratched his bottom.

Cudweed took that as a 'yes'.

'Excellent!' cried Cudweed.

Soon the ship was ready, and
Cudweed and Fellah climbed aboard,
shaking lots of tentacles, and saying
lots of thank-yous.

'Right, Fellah, time for blast off!
Stand back there, Thrillons!' he cried.

They shot off into space.

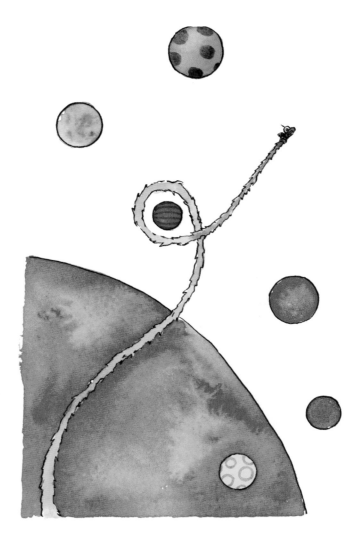

'What nice people,' Cudweed said as they headed home. 'When you get to know them. But they could have offered us a piece of cake.'

Luckily, it was teatime in the castle when Cudweed and Fellah got home, and soon they got stuck into cakes and biscuits and scones and jam.

Cudweed's dad arrived a little later.

'What's wrong?' Cudweed asked.
His dad looked grumpy.

'Well, my boy,' he said. 'I've been
trying to invent a spaceship all day so
that I can explore outer space, and it
just won't work.'

'If I were you,' said Cudweed.
'I wouldn't bother. Nothing very
exciting happens.'

He winked at Fellah, and helped
himself to another slice of cake.

Also by Marcus Sedgwick
and Pete Williamson

CUDWEED'S BIRTHDAY

978 1 4440 0319 2
£4.99